Strawberry Fairchild AND THE GREEN FLAME

A Fable by Alan Mark Train
Illustrated by Mari Yamagiwa

WRITERS BOOK FAIR

ISBN: 978-1-962313-29-2 (Paperback)
ISBN: 978-1-962313-30-8 (Hardback)
ISBN: 978-1-962313-28-5 (eBook)

Book Ordering Information

Writers Book Fair
99 Wall Street Suite 181
New York, NY, 10005, USA

info@writersbookfair.com
www.writersbookfair.com

Printed in the United States of America

CONTENTS

Acknowledgments

Clown image on back cover by Sandra Forslund.

Thank you to Amy Russell and team, brother Bob, Uncle Arty, Fran Farley, Evan Miller, Karl Nielsen, David Porter, Toni Danilevsky and Beardog for their feedback and support. And to Grace and the Internet for bringing Author and Illustrator together.

Preface

"Well, she's walking through the clouds
With a circus mind that's running round
Butterflies and zebras
And moonbeams and fairy tales
That's all she ever thinks about
Riding with the wind."

- Jimi Hendrix, **Little Wing**

"On the western hills the sun sets, the eastern hills darken, horses blown by the whirlwind tread the clouds. From colored lute and plain pipes, crowd faint notes: her flowered skirt rustles as she steps in the autumn dust. When the wind brushes the cassia leaves and a cassia seed drops The blue raccoon weeps blood and the cold fox dies. Dragons painted on the ancient wall with tails of inlaid gold The God of Rain rides into the autumn pool; and the owl a hundred years old, which changed to a goblin of the trees, hears the sound of laughter as GREEN FLAMES *start up inside its nest…"*

- Li Ho, 8th century Chinese poet (translated by A. C. Graham), **A Piece for Magic Strings**

PROLOGUE

From flippers to slippers
Some tinge to rose.
From slipknots to fishnets
The rolling of fins
Whisper a clothing of shows.

scene one

Near blackest night, sight of white surf.
Blue ocean, where moonlit silver blue.

Far off sound of dolphins gradually grows nearer.
Sound stops. Momentary total darkness.

Then laughter, girlish, and a voice likewise:
“Hey guys, hey dolphins, don’t go!”

Receding splashing sounds are heard.
“They really did it.”

Scene Two

Nearby, same near blackest night.
Yellow-lit windows of a small town hospital's maternity ward.

Voices, mingled, a loud sneeze, the lights flash briefly.
A thump, voices, distinct now:

"A catastrophe!"
"My word but he's absurd."

"Can't we keep him dear?"
"Nope. It hurts the sinus (your highness). It's been a while since I saw this happen but I know what should be done."

"What can we do?"

"What we did the last time."

Consequently…

Scene Three

Guided by porpoise-full wisdom, Strawberry transforms the little gray whale-child into the Sweet Pig and remarks of the transformation:

"Maybe not attractive to the gourmet, but he's tasteful enough and to me a real treat!"

Enter Zooney in zoot suit, Strawberry's heretofore unheard of cousin. He is behind the wheel of his orange-colored convertible with the cranberry-red top, creamy whitewalls, almond steering wheel and mint-tinted windshield.

Strawberry (to Zooney): "Were you left by the dolphins too?"

Zooney: "How did you guess?"

Strawberry: "Do you have to return to them when your porpoise is complete?"

Zooney: "No Strawberry. I'm not graceful enough."

Scene Four

Strawberry is scandalized and The Sweet Pig implicated. Her success as a magician and a modern dancer spur the jealous to rage.

It becomes known that the young gentleman seen accompanying her of late is not a stranger but the whale-child discarded in winter.

They place Strawberry under house arrest, citing her oceanic origin and the absurd birth of her playmate as justification. (A sleazy effort to ruin her.)

Ring. Ring.
"From whence came this elvish seachild?"

Ring. Ring. Ring.
"And from what womb sprang this Sweet Pig?"

Scene Five

Zooney splits but The Sweet Pig sneaks in for a visit.

Sweet Pig: "Natasha, we have to stop meeting like this!"

Strawberry: "Very funny but my sense of porpoise tells me we must seek the aid of the elusive **GREEN FLAME**. Since I am under house arrest, it is you who must find him!"

The Sweet Pig: "How will I know for sure that it's him Strawberry?"

Strawberry:
"His is a precious beam that shows no seam
and behind that beam is the gleam
of a flame that's **GREEN***."*

The Sweet Pig exits, reciting:
"Stalking, stealing, trailing,
Murmuring a name,
Deft and darkened,
Chasing the sleek **GREEN FLAME***."*

That night he makes his bed in a ravine by the side of the road.

An Officer awakes The Sweet Pig out of his sleep:
"You, Pig, on your feet."

"I have been disturbing no peaks."

"Peace. Disturbing the peace."

"Well I have not."

"Okay, who cares anyway? You seen an Emerald Bull around here?"

Green

Scene Six

The next morning he isn't far down the road when he runs into what seems a pleasant enough fellow, The Emerald Bull.

And a Stranger joins them out of nowhere:
"Howdy."

The Sweet Pig:
"Yo. People are strange when you're a stranger and I've always trusted in the kindness of strangers."

The Emerald Bull leads the three of them through landscape increasingly shadowed.

The Sweet Pig (uncomfortably): "It's gettin' shadowy. My oscillating self-image is acting up."

The Emerald Bull: "Further, never straight? Look in front of you but scintillate sideways."

They soon encounter a cheap double parading as THE GREEN FLAME, The Limelight. Some foolish moments ensue before the thinness of this illusion becomes apparent.

The Stranger: "Is that The Limelight flashing just beyond the horizon?"

The Sweet Pig: "Perhaps no more than a pigment of your imagination."

The Emerald Bull: "You mean, I bet, figment."

The Stranger (impatiently): "Who cares what the pig meant. Let's get going."

scene seven

All his stalking, all his stealing and trailing, even all name murmuring, prove in vain. THE FLAME continues to elude him, and later that same day he falls into the clutches of The Dire Wolf.

Before leaving to make preparations for a taste of the boy, The Wolf ties him around the waist to a wooden chair facing a barred window. The Sweet Pig can see the sunny day outside.

The Wolf has also ordered that a television set be left blaring. It can be heard throughout the scene.

The Sweet Pig can't even hear himself think: "I can't even hear myself think."

In dire distress he gazes out the window, through his pain:
"I miss you Strawberry. Badly, I miss you badly."

Some few sad minutes pass. Suddenly struck (by an idea) he plunges his right hand into his back pocket, rummages through it, finds three crumpled balloons: one purple, one yellow and one blue.

He blows them up, again searches the pocket, finds an orange crayon and scrawls "HELP!" in huge letters across all three. Meanwhile The Wolf's servants have set up a large cauldron, which can be seen boiling actively.

The Sweet Pig takes his balloons and, one at a time, attempts to push them through the bars. The first two burst but the blue one makes it without exploding, catches the wind, and sails out of sight.

The TV begins playing food commercials. Seeing the cauldron for the first time, The Sweet Pig exclaims: "The seals have my fate."

Then he faints.

Scene Eight

Summary?

The Sweet Pig meets THE GREEN FLAME in a dream and wakes to find a remnant of the scene.

Black stage with flame (GREEN FLAME) backdrop, single spotlight.

A figure in a GREEN costume splattered with words in bold black letters enters from the left and dances until he reaches center stage. He's wearing a white hat with black feathers. Suddenly, to his surprise, a number of large cardboard words fall from his pocket onto the stage floor.

The frustrated dancer-mime, obviously THE GREEN FLAME, annoyed, stoops to pick them up and again begins dancing. After a few steps, he stumbles on a cardboard word he had neglected to pick up. He grabs it and holds it up to view. It reads, in big letters, "SPLASH."

At the end of this sequence, the figure brilliantly charades the mysterious object required for The Sweet Pig's escape.

scene nine

The Sweet Pig awakes, or rather materializes, near the ocean and nowhere near The Wolf's den. He finds the object mimed by THE FLAME lying at his feet – an autographed copy of James Joyce's Ulysses. He also finds Strawberry and Zooney waiting for him.

The Sweet Pig stares down at the book:
"Ahh, fiction, a relief. I can only live with so much friction."

And then looks over at Strawberry and Zoon: "I love you Strawberry, madly. I love you madly."

Zooney: "Where did he come from?"

The Sweet Pig: "It matters not from what womb I sprang."

Strawberry: "He means, maybe, room."

The Sweet Pig: "Yes, yes I did. By the way I'm not chicken, Strawberry, but this whole business of paying dues to The Wolf just makes me sad."

Strawberry looks over at Zooney imploringly.

Zooney: "We're glad to rescue you, Pig, but there's something we need to tell you as well. I need to split again, which shouldn't bother you too much, but Strawberry too is leaving, returning to the dolphins and the ocean. You'll have to carry on without her."

Sweet Pig: "Good time for a smack of pokes!"

Strawberry nudges Zooney: "Please give The Sweet P a cigarette."

The Sweet Pig (after first lighting up): "I, then, shall disappear into mist."

Strawberry: “For goodness sake, you mean myth, Sweet.”

Then, blushing: “Speaking of which, I hear the dolphins.”

Zooney: “I don’t.”

Strawberry: “Far off. I hear them.”

Sweet Pig: “You’re being flippant, Strawberry.”

Strawberry: “No. Flippered.”

The Sweet Pig:
“Makes my heart leap but no matter. Deep breaths and on, words, word load and all…

Bright curtains slip through needles’ eyes in threads.
Let me put it in verse:

‘Crossways of thought
Don’t like to be lost
And bright thread slips
Through needles’ eyes
In ribbons.’”

SCOTCH
SCOTCH WHISKY
ESTABLISHED
1878

Scene Ten

Surf, sand, and seashells as far as they could see. And it wasn't fantasy – it was really dusk, dusk and white surf.

The Stranger shows up unexpectedly, out of nowhere as always. He gets introduced to Strawberry and Zooney and asks: "Where y'all goin?"

The Sweet Pig: "Me, I'm gonna pursue other angels."

The Stranger: "You mean angles, right?"

Sweet Pig: "No. I mean angels."

Stranger: "Sweet Pig, did it ever occur to you that what you ought best to pursue is your own writing?"

Sweet Pig (bows and recites):
"In THE GREEN FLAME'S *web caught*
He offered her his earthly thought.
She offered him her hands and spine,
Grace, dignity and sense of line."

Strawberry points out that although she will be gone this 'sense of line' belongs to both her and The Sweet Pig.

The Sweet Pig, very moved, turns to her:
"The language of love is the language of dance.
My language is the language of friends —
Refracted pebbles of shattered glass flowers,
And prisms viewed askance,
Glanced on lips and fingertips,
Born for a child of chance."

Zooney: “Later.”

Sweet Pig:

“Hand waves in jest,
Whirls about,
Gestures at blessed,
Unstuck hand
Amidst jester and guest.”

EPILOGUE

Vanishing ocean sounds continue from the previous scene. A boy, one who looks much like The Sweet Pig, awakes and sits up in his bed, grabbing the brass rail of the bedpost with both hands. He stares out the window at the same ocean revealed by the opening curtain.

Then he softly whispers to himself:

"Slipping through the seaweed
Towards the golden shore,
I sometimes lose my footing
On the ocean floor.

My hats get wet
Playing the deep GREEN *game*
Of searching the seashell,
Calling your name."

www.ingramcontent.com/pod-product-compliance
Ingram Content Group UK Ltd.
Pitfield, Milton Keynes, MK11 3LW, UK
UKHW050142280726
14058UKWH00006B/783